New Life: New Room

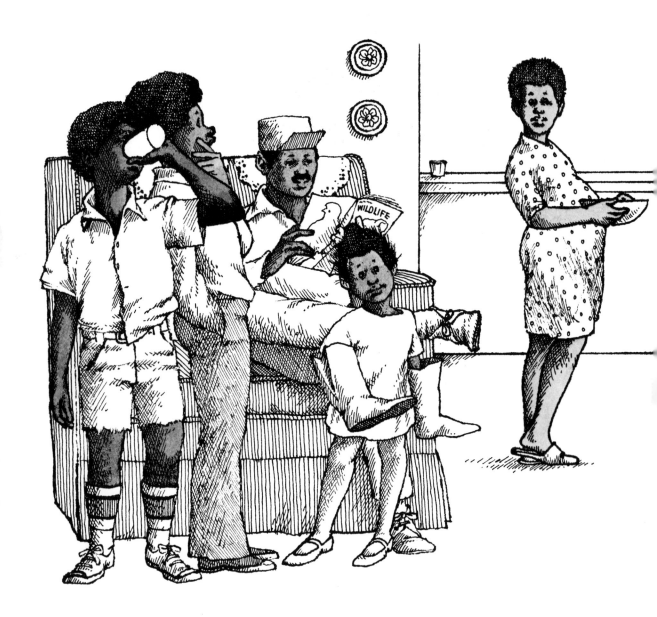

New Life: New Room

BY JUNE JORDAN

Illustrated by Ray Cruz

Thomas Y. Crowell Company
New York

Also by June Jordan

Who Look at Me
His Own Where
Fannie Lou Hamer

Library of Congress Cataloging in Publication Data
Jordan, June, date   New Life: New Room.
SUMMARY: Encouraged by Father, three children move into and decorate
their own room while Mother is in the hospital having a new baby sister.
[1. Brothers and sisters—Fiction. 2. Family life—Fiction] I. Ray Cruz, illus.
II. Title.
PZ7.J763Ne3   [Fic]   73-9755
ISBN 0-690-00211-4   ISBN 0-690-00212-2 (lib. bdg.)

1   2   3   4   5   6   7   8   9   10

For Wendy Because

New Life: New Room

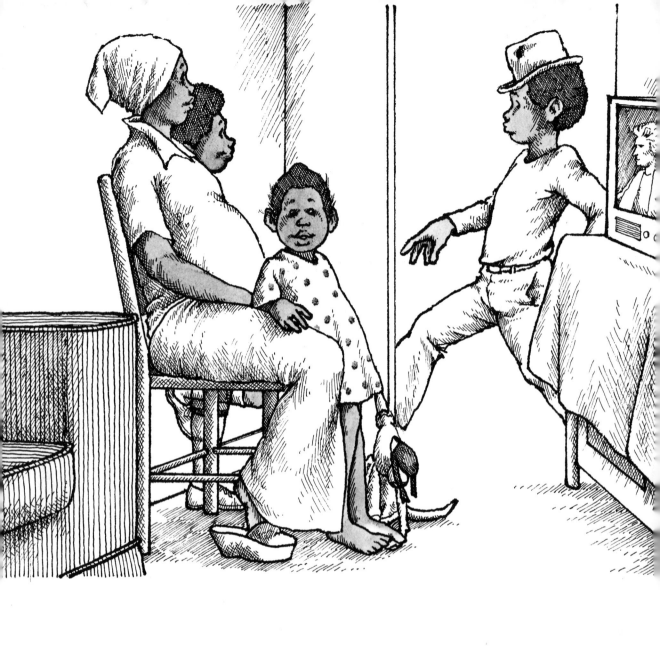

1

On top of Momma getting so big and so sleepy, the apartment was beginning to be small.

This wasn't happening right away, but it was happening too soon. Rudy, Tyrone, and Linda were not ready for a small house. But they had to get ready because, if they didn't, one night, the new baby would come home, suddenly, with no warning, and that would be that. The apartment would be too small.

They had to hurry up, but they didn't know how. "Could be nice," Linda kept on saying, in the talks she and her brothers kept on having. "Could be cozy." "Cozy!" Both of her brothers broke up, giggling and laughing at the idea.

In a way, they were scared about the new baby. In a way they were angry about the house getting so much smaller all the time. In a way they felt funny because they didn't feel sure about anything anymore.

Rudy Robinson was ten years old—the oldest, in fact—and he knew the most about what a new baby could mean. He could never forget when Tyrone came into the picture. That was when Momma got lost in the hospital, for days. Mr. Robinson, Rudy's daddy, and Aunts, and neighbors, kissed Rudy, or carried him outdoors, or came to feed and then to bathe him with large, purple soap bubbles floating in the water, but nothing was the same.

Rudy remembered crying, but he remembered that the crying did not change anything. Momma went right ahead, staying away, until she finally came back, with Tyrone, who never left the family, after that.

"Your Baby Brother," people called Tyrone.

Sometimes Tyrone acted deaf because so many folks had this terrible habit of calling him Baby Brother, even now—and he was just about as tall as Rudy.

For example, Mr. Robinson might say: "Rudy, when you go to the store, why don't you take Baby Brother with you?" Tyrone thought that his father probably loved him, Tyrone, but, now and again, he would wonder about it: Why doesn't he call me by my name?

That was a strange thing about grown-ups. They would say *the children,* or they would say *your father,* or they would say, *"How's my Baby Girl?"*

Linda really was the baby, and she really was a girl. Since Rudy was ten, and Tyrone was nine, she was the youngest one, at six years old, no question about it. But Linda didn't understand this Baby Girl business, either. Rudy thought Tyrone and Linda were stupid, or at other times, he thought they were silly, to worry about names so much. He tried to make them laugh about it, but they refused, absolutely, to laugh.

When somebody's mother yelled out of a project window, way up high in the building, "Where's Baby Brother?" maybe fifteen different kids would feel the words striking on their own ears, hard. (My baby brother? Me? Whose baby brother?)

Anyway, the point was that a new Baby Brother or a new Baby Girl was coming into the Robinson apartment, any minute, and what would happen then? Rudy said that wasn't the point at all. Tyrone and Linda would simply gain a regular name—like *Rudy*.

What was very much in doubt was something else. How was the apartment going to hold Mr. Robinson, Mrs. Robinson, Rudy, Tyrone, Linda, *and* a new Baby Brother, or a new Baby Girl?

"It'll be crowded," said Mr. Robinson, shaking his head. He looked over at his wife: "I wish the housing people would let us have a bigger place. I honestly do. But they don't

6

let you have a reason to hope. They just tell you they're sorry, they're sorry."

Mrs. Robinson heard how the voice of her husband was tired. She put her hand on his arm, and smiled. "Look. We don't need a bigger place," she said, "we just have to use our heads."

"Honey, your head and my head put together don't give us another room. But okay. Let's not talk about it."

"Well, I've been thinking," said Mrs. Rob-

inson. "Linda can't go on sleeping in the living room. How about her moving in with the boys?"

"That's fine with me, so long as you're the one to break the bad news to the boys," answered Mr. Robinson. But when he saw little worry lines getting tight around the eyes of his wife, he stopped teasing and said, "That's the way it has to be, that's the way it'll be. We'll work it out."

"But I won't be here to help!" said Mrs. Robinson.

"Listen," her husband continued, "it's going to be their room, right? So the best thing is for them to figure it out by themselves. Then we'll just do what we can, when they ask us. How does that sound?"

"Sounds too easy." Mrs. Robinson laughed. "With you away at work and me away at the hospital. You know they're just babies and not a one of them anybody you can call neat!"

Mr. Robinson joined her laughing. "You

put our three kids in one, single, solitary room, and you can be sure nobody's going to be neat. But there is one thing we can do, to get them started," he said, leaning on his elbows, and speaking more slowly. "While you're in the hospital, I'll take everything out of our bedroom, and bring the children's things in there, so at least they can have a bigger playpen, or whatever it will turn out to be."

Mrs. Robinson looked relieved, and then excited. "Of course!" she said, beginning to smile. "We'll switch rooms with the children. There will be plenty of space for our bed in the boys' room if we put the baby's crib—"

"Hold everything!" said Mr. Robinson. "You sound like you're moving the furniture. We'll move everything while you're resting in the hospital. Let it be a surprise to you."

"Oh, Lord!" said Mrs. Robinson, "let it be a *happy* surprise for all of us!"

And that was how the answer began to come up to the question about more room for the growing Robinson family.

2

Linda couldn't understand. No matter who told her, again and again, she couldn't understand why she had to give up her place.

At first, Linda had been very unhappy, years before, when she had to move out from her parents' bedroom, and when she had to take over the living-room couch as her own bed. But soon she learned how to open and close the couch up easily. And then she got used to hanging her clothes in the hallway closet, or folding them for the bottom drawer of her mother's bureau, or pushing them into the skinny top drawer of her brothers' bureau. So she began to really like her place in the apartment. It was interesting to have parts of you spread out or hiding everywhere,

all over the whole house. And it was fun to sleep in the big double bed belonging to her mother and father sometimes, whenever there was company or a party going on.

And in some ways, the living room was the best because everybody came into it, every day, and because that was where the family would just sit, talking, or else dance, or else watch the TV. There was no loneliness in the living room. So it was a good part, and maybe the best part, of the house.

Her brothers, Rudy and Tyrone, thought they understood, but still they didn't like the idea. They liked Linda okay. But they didn't like the idea of giving up their places, either. They didn't like the idea of moving out of their own room where they had spent so many nights and days whispering and planning things and playing games.

And that was another problem. What about

Linda's toys? Would she have to bring them into the new room?

Tyrone thought that all girl toys were corny or dumb or boring. Rudy only thought they were boring, but he could see how Linda liked some of them, so he never said anything, out loud.

But Tyrone was worried. "Suppose she brings in the dolls, and the doll carriage, and the stove that doesn't even get hot or anything?"

"So?" answered Rudy, looking around. "How are they going to bother you?"

"That's what I mean," said Tyrone. "You

can't even be bothered about them. All her girl toys are the same. They all look like grown-up work. Like babies or cooking. Old things you supposed to do. What fun is that supposed to be?"

"Yeah," Rudy agreed, "but it's not her fault. She can't help it if she's a girl and people keep giving her crazy presents like that."

Tyrone was quiet for a minute. Then he said, "Maybe we should make a deal."

"Like what?"

"Like no toys, no games, no nothing, unless all Three of us want to use it, you know. Nothing stays unless we all like it. Unless we can all use it for real."

"I don't know," said Rudy. "Linda is so little. And you and I don't even like the same things all the time."

"Well, but we could try, couldn't we?"

"Okay. We could try," answered Rudy.

16

"Anyhow, that way we get to throw out a whole lot of junk. Or give it away."

"Yeah. And I hate junk," said Tyrone.

"Oh," said Rudy, "you hate everything and everybody."

"I do not."

"You do so," Rudy said, bringing his face up close to his brother's face.

"I don't," answered Tyrone, pushing his brother away from him.

"You do!" said Rudy, punching Tyrone on the arm.

And then Rudy and Tyrone got into a fight that broke three toys and busted up two games, so that there was going to be less junk to get rid of, little by little.

3

Finally, Mr. and Mrs. Robinson called the children together. They said this and that. But mostly, Rudy, Tyrone, and Linda understood that Momma would have to leave for the hospital any minute: tonight, even, or the next day; and while she was gone, they would all have to get ready, and help, and move things around, and lose places and trade places in the house.

It was going to be terrible. That was clear.

But actually Mr. and Mrs. Robinson said many things. They said the new baby would cry in the night, maybe for hours, and somebody would have to walk UP and DOWN to calm the baby. They said somebody would have to get up in the night and cross through the living room to reach the kitchen to heat the milk for the baby. They said that somebody would have to open the refrigerator, and fool with doors, and run water, and stir things with spoons making a noise against glass, and turn on and then off and then on and then off the lights in the living room and the kitchen. They said they would have to keep a light on in the living room, so nobody would trip and fall on the way to the kitchen. And they said Mrs. Robinson would have to try and quiet the new baby in the living room, so that Mr. Robinson could sleep in the bedroom and be rested for work the next day.

19

That was what they said.

Then Mrs. Robinson left for the hospital, and by the next morning, the new baby, a new Baby Girl, had been born.

4

Mr. Robinson had been awake all night long, at the hospital. When the new Baby Girl was born, he was happy, and tired, and he took the day off from work. He felt he needed to celebrate, visit his wife, look at his new Baby Girl, take care of Rudy, Tyrone, Linda, move furniture, and sleep.

First he went to sleep. Then, when he woke

up, he worked for two hours with a neighbor who was a friend of his. His friend gave him a cigar, a friendly, loud slap on the back, and a good, strong, helping hand.

Together they pushed, pulled, lifted, turned, and made things bump, slide, roll, scrape, bang, and rock from one room to the other.

In the middle of this, the children came home from school.

They were shocked.

They felt excited and scared and strange and crowded and lonely and pleased to see the terrific mess the two men were making in the house.

Momma was certainly gone.

After Mr. Robinson stopped moving things and after he and his friend finished two beers, they left for the hospital. But just before he went out the door, Mr. Robinson tried to hug Rudy and Tyrone and Linda, in one big hug, with his huge, strong arms. But he couldn't quite do that, so he kissed each of them, in turn.

He said, "I'll be back soon, and I'll bring in some dinner by the time you're hungry. . . . But meanwhile, why don't you go ahead and start trying out your new room?"

Then Mr. Robinson went away.

5

Now they were alone. The old house seemed new. Their new room didn't look right. For one thing, there were only two beds for the three of them. Where was Linda going to sleep?

Besides everything else, the new room looked too big. Rudy's narrow cot was up against one wall. Tyrone's narrow cot was on the other side of the room, against another wall. Between them, in the middle of the floor, was a trunk full of toys. And next to the closet, their bureau looked big and lumpy and old.

All three children felt shy and small. Then Linda began running around. She brought all of her toys and threw them on top of the trunk. Next she brought all of her clothes out from every hiding place in the house and threw them on top of the toys.

Rudy went into action, and he began taking out the drawers from the bureau and dumping all of his and Tyrone's clothes on top of Linda's. Tyrone rushed after them, piling up games on top of clothes on top of toys on top of the trunk in the middle of the floor.

So the room began to look better. It didn't look too big anymore. But the two beds were still far apart. You couldn't whisper from one bed to the other. So Tyrone and Rudy and Linda pulled the cots close by the mountain of things in the middle of the floor, and made the two cots into something like a long, low table.

That was where the children were playing cards, and sitting and laughing and having a good time, when Mr. Robinson came home from the hospital with Aunt Valerie, Mrs. Robinson's sister, who wanted to be helpful.

The grown-ups opened the door to the new room and Aunt Valerie said:

"OH."

Aunt Valerie usually talked a lot. So Rudy, Tyrone, and Linda knew she must be upset because she couldn't seem to say anything more.

"This is the new room for the children," said Mr. Robinson.

"OH. What a shame," said Aunt Valerie, staring at the mountain of toys and clothes.

"We're starting to share things," said Rudy, opening his eyes wide.

"Well," said Mr. Robinson, taking a deep breath, "it'll be hard to know whose is what, the way things are, don't you think?"

Tyrone stood up, and walked over to lean himself under his father's arm: "We don't need to know, do we, Daddy?" he asked.

"Maybe not," said Mr. Robinson, resting his hand, lightly, on the top of Tyrone's head.

But Aunt Valerie couldn't stand it. "Why don't you kids go and watch television for half an hour, and let me just straighten everything out for you," she said moving into the room suddenly.

"Well, wait, now," said Mr. Robinson, in a friendly way. "You see, we sort of decided that the children would take care of their room themselves, and the grown-ups would stay on the sidelines unless we were asked to come in."

"All right!" said Aunt Valerie, with a

slightly sharp ring to her voice, "I can tell when I'm not wanted."

"Oh, come on!" laughed Mr. Robinson. "I want you to keep me company in the kitchen, while I heat up some of this food I bought."

Then he led Aunt Valerie out of the room.

"Whew," said Tyrone.

"Wow," said Linda. "I hope Daddy gets me a bed tomorrow, so this is the last night I will have to sleep in the living room, with Aunt Valerie and everything."

"What do you think?" asked Rudy.

"I think we better keep the door closed until Aunt Valerie goes away," Tyrone announced.

And so they did.

6

There was hardly any time left. Today was when Linda would begin to sleep, as well as play, in the same room with her brothers. Then the next day after this one was when Momma and the new Baby Girl would come home from the hospital.

Mr. Robinson bought a camp cot for Linda, and three jars of poster paint, yellow, red, and blue. Then, from his pockets he took out three thin paintbrushes. But under his chin, and inside his arms, was a gallon of chocolate ripple and strawberry ice cream, for the celebration.

Everybody was excited, and talking at once.

"What's the paint for?" asked Linda.

"I thought you kids would find something to do with it, in your new room," said Mr. Robinson.

"The windows!" shouted Tyrone. "We can paint the windows like a church or something!"

"That'll be pretty when the sun comes through," said Aunt Valerie.

"Well," said Mr. Robinson, "it *will* be pretty, if you mix the paints with water, so it won't be too thick. And don't worry," he smiled at Aunt Valerie. "Poster paint washes right off. No problem there."

But the children were already inside their new room, arguing and trying to start.

Rudy took the blue, and Tyrone took the yellow, and Linda took the red paint.

They couldn't agree on the drawing, or the designs for the window. And there was a silence.

But then Rudy said, "Why don't we race, I mean, like on your mark, get ready, and paint! And we'll just race through one window and then do the other one, but we'll have

to be racing each other to get our own color on the windows—What do you say?"

Tyrone and Linda were choosing up positions next to Rudy at the first window.

Elbows pointed together sharp and bony as Rudy called out: "On your mark! Get ready! *Paint!!*"

And they were off, painting, bumping, spilling, dabbing, dripping, poking, streaming, splashing, red and yellow and blue over the glass.

It got to be very interesting.

After a few minutes they stopped and looked. In fact, the window was beginning to look good, all right. But there was a lot of purple and a lot of green where the colors ran together.

So the children slowed down, a bit, and began to move out of each other's way, so that red or yellow or blue could take its place on the window pane and make shapes that were smiling, round, happy, large shapes of color that the sunlight would turn to warm and burning color rays like a rainbow bright over the whole room.

Then they rested the paint jars and brushes on the floor and stood still, considering what to do next.

Rudy said, "Let's get the toys and stuff sorted out and decide who gets to keep what, so we all can use all of the things, and then we can paint the top of the trunk too, if we feel like it."

So they scrambled into the great, tumbling pile of things and began to call out:

"Doll!"

"Throw!"

"Flashlight!"

"Keep!"

"Gun!"

"Throw!"

"Helmet!"

"Keep!"

"Stove!"

"Throw!"

"Tank!"

"Throw!"

"Magnets!"

"Keep!"

"Comic books!"

"Keep!"

"Dice!"

"Keep!"

"Rope!"

"Keep!"

"Blocks!"
"*Throw!*"
"*Keep!*"
"*Throw!*"

Linda wanted them thrown out. She wanted to get rid of everything babyish.

But Tyrone loved his blocks: "You just don't know what to do with blocks," he said. "You never built anything in your life!"

"You never let me," answered Linda.

"Well, now you can," Rudy observed. "We'll show you how. You could try building a house. That's easy."

Linda thought. "Do you know how to take care of a baby?"

"Oh, quit that," said Rudy. "A doll isn't anybody's baby."

"So what? Your blocks are make-believe too," she pointed out.

"Yeah. But what's more important? Building a bridge or taking care of a baby?" asked Tyrone.

"The baby," Linda said right away.

"What do you think?" Tyrone turned to Rudy.

But Rudy shrugged his shoulders and wouldn't say anything.

So Tyrone looked angry, but he kept quiet.

"I only want one doll," said Linda, sitting down, cross-legged, on the floor. "Just one. And you can play with her if you want."

Tyrone was making his mind up, slowly. At last he said, "That's the deal. All right. Keep the blocks and keep the doll. One doll. And I get to keep my robot. The man from Mars that broke so easy."

So they went ahead, and finished sorting the toys. Then they made several trips down the hall to friends' houses, and threw out the things nobody wanted anymore in the incinerator.

Now everything would fit inside the trunk.

And they closed it up, and painted three, big, overlapping circles, red, yellow, and blue, to cover the whole top of the dark green trunk.

Things were looking up.

"What about that big old bureau?" Tyrone asked aloud.

"Well, what about it?" asked Rudy.

"How can we hide it somewhere so we don't have to see it—so it's not sticking up ugly like that?"

At this moment, Mr. Robinson came into the room, and laughed, delighted with all the colors, and all the work done so fast.

"Hey, you kids have done a great job here,"

he told them. "Everything's going to be fine!"

"Tyrone wants to throw out the bureau," Linda said, still a bit angry at Tyrone because she was only going to get to keep one doll.

But nobody could talk Mr. Robinson into throwing out the whole bureau, even though Rudy and Tyrone tried hard.

"I'll tell you what," said Mr. Robinson. "Leave the drawers out, but push them under the bed. One under each cot. That way they'll stay out of your way. And if you paint them different colors, you won't get them mixed up. How's that?"

Before anyone could answer, he carried the bureau frame out of the room, and out of sight.

So that solved the problem of the bureau that had been sticking up too high, too wide, and too ugly, in the new space of the new room.

42

7

"Isn't it time for you children to take a bath?" called Aunt Valerie.

"Okay," said Linda.

"Okay," said Tyrone.

"Right away," said Rudy.

And the three children stripped and ran to the bathroom and closed the door and filled the tub with water and all tried to squeeze into the same tub at the same time.

But this proved to be impossible, and Tyrone and Linda and Rudy got into a laughing fit that turned into a tickle fight that sloshed great waves of water onto the floor.

"Now just a minute!" said Mr. Robinson, banging into the bathroom. "You know better than this," he said. "I'll give you four and a half minutes to put this bathroom back to rights, the way you found it, clean, AND DRY," he said, and banged out of the bathroom as suddenly as he had come.

Rudy, Tyrone, and Linda looked at each other. Daddy was *mad.* So they huddled close together, and whispered, and tried not to giggle anymore, and wrapped themselves in towels and tried not to shiver, and Rudy went and got a mop and all the children struggled to meet the four and a half minute clean-up deadline set by Mr. Robinson. Then they sneaked back to their new room, and got into pajamas and slippers, and made up their

44

beds for the night, and came out to the living room.

Mr. Robinson looked over at them, from the TV program he was watching with Aunt Valerie.

"Well. All set?" he asked. Then, seeing how nervously and stiff they were standing to-

gether, he felt sorry for having lost his temper in the bathroom.

So he went over to them and brought their heads together, inside his arms, and kissed them.

"Tonight's a big night for you, isn't it?" he said in his deep voice. "You're all going to sleep in your new room for the first time. How about some strawberry and chocolate ripple ice cream, before you go to bed?"

At the table, Mr. Robinson asked the children what else they would like to have for the new room, and the children all said they would like something alive like goldfish or some baby plants that they could take care of, and help to grow.

It was like a party. A pajama party with ice cream and soda and Daddy and Aunt Valerie and a brand-new room that would look like a rainbow in the morning.

46

8

When they got into bed, nobody said a word for two minutes. The new room felt new. There was nothing but darkness. Somebody moved and made peculiar, quick noises. Then a flashlight went on, making a shadowy circle on the ceiling.

"Is anybody awake?" Tyrone whispered.

"Me," said Linda.

"Me too," said Rudy.

"I don't like it," Linda said.

"What?"

"The room. Everything's so far apart. How can we talk without Daddy hearing us? We'll get into trouble," said Linda.

"Well," Rudy said, "let's bring our cots together, over here by the windows, away from the door."

The children tiptoed around in the flashlight, and pulled the three cots together, side

by side. But then they got the giggles again, and started to tickle each other and the cots began to slide and shake and pull apart. So Rudy got up and went to find some rope, to tie the cots together. But he went looking without a flashlight, and smashed his toes into the trunk still standing in the center of the room, where the paint was drying on it.

Rudy felt the tears running from his eyes. His toes hurt. The pain was terrible. And now Tyrone and Linda could hear him crying.

They got up, and brought him back to his cot, limping badly. Tyrone tied the beds together with the rope. And the three children snuggled together, on their new, big bed, in their new big room, that was full of darkness.

Snuggling made Rudy stop crying, and the children laughed and talked and scared each other and then calmed each other down for almost a whole hour more, before they all fell asleep at last.

9

Morning came with sunlight, and red and yellow and blue colors striped and circled the new room where the children lay, waking up, slowly.

It was a beautiful day. It was a beautiful room, very big, and open, and Rudy and Tyrone and Linda felt they were a bunch of lucky people—lucky to live together this way.

Rudy was not alone. Tyrone was not alone. And Linda was not alone. They were together in their own room. And they called it OUR ROOM.

And Momma would be coming back today.
And a new Baby Girl was coming with her.
And everything was okay.
And everyone was ready.

About the Author

June Jordan is a poet, novelist, and teacher, and the author of several distinguished books for children: *Who Look at Me, His Own Where,* and *Fannie Lou Hamer.* Born in New York City, she studied at Barnard College and the University of Chicago, and has taught at the City College of New York, Connecticut College, Sarah Lawrence College, and Yale University. She is a cofounder of a creative writing workshop for Black and Puerto Rican teen-agers in Brooklyn. Two collections of her own poems have been published, and she is the editor of two anthologies of Afro-American poetry. An adult novel, *Okay Now,* will appear in the fall of 1975. The recipient of a Rockefeller Foundation fellowship in creative writing and of the Prix de Rome in environmental design, Ms. Jordan now lives in Brooklyn and divides her time between teaching at Yale and writing.

About the Artist

Ray Cruz was born and lives in New York City. He studied art at the High School of Art and Design and at Pratt Institute, and was graduated from Cooper Union. Mr. Cruz has illustrated many books for children, and as a commercial artist has designed everything from packages to murals. His special interests are wildlife conservation and environmental protection, and he is an active member of many organizations devoted to these causes.